THE BLACK COUGARS

BOOK 1

Abby Hatch

authorHOUSE®

AuthorHouse™
1663 Liberty Drive
Bloomington, IN 47403
www.authorhouse.com
Phone: 1 (800) 839-8640

Published by AuthorHouse 07/25/2019

ISBN: 978-1-7283-1730-4 (sc)
ISBN: 978-1-7283-1728-1 (hc)
ISBN: 978-1-7283-1729-8 (e)

Library of Congress Control Number: 2019908551

Print information available on the last page.

This book is printed on acid-free paper.

To all of my middle school friends. Without my middle school friend group, this story would not be possible.

CHAPTER ONE

M Y NAME IS LAUREN. I am fifteen years old. My friends call me - well that's not important right now. What's important is that I tell you what happened to get me here, with these people. This is my story.

One day I was walking home from school on some railroad tracks. It was about 3:45. I was wearing a lilac tank dress that came down to my knees with shiny black shoes and light gray leggings. My black hair was flowing down my tie-dye backpack and I was listening to Katy Perry with my white earbuds.

I was just minding my own business, walking along the tracks, looking at the clouds in the sky with my brown eyes, when a flash of movement out of the corner of my eye caught my attention. I stopped walking and took one earbud out.

"Hello?" I called out. "Is anyone there?"

No response.

I continued walking cautiously with one earbud out. It occurred to me that I had never taken this route before. I kept walking cautiously.

Suddenly, two boys of about sixteen wearing black leather jackets, white shirts, and black jeans came up and grabbed me by the arms. Both of them were blonde, but one of them was a dirty blonde with hazel eyes and a dragon tattoo on the left side of his neck, and the other had brown hair near the bottom and blonde on the top with brown eyes. He was wearing a black bandana tied around his forehead.

"Hey!" I screamed, struggling to break free. "Let me go!" They put me into the back of a yellow classic convertible and both got into the front. We drove for a while until the sun started to set. Then, the car stopped and the boys got out and grabbed me again. We walked for about fifteen minutes, and I was struggling the whole time.

We finally got to an area where a group of kids that were about sixteen to seventeen were standing near a fire in a trash can. It was dark by the time we got there. There was an old, beaten up, rusty truck sitting next to them. They were laughing, and then they looked up at me and my captors. They were all wearing the same thing as the boys who took me.

One of the boys in the group looked about seventeen. He had ginger hair that swept to the side so his left eye was covered. He had freckles and hazel eyes. He had a tiny gold hoop earring (like the one that Mr. Clean wears) in his right earlobe and a lollipop stick in his mouth. He turned to the people who took me as they brought me into the clearing.

"Blade, Mangle. Let the poor girl go."

They looked at me with disgust and reluctantly took their hands off of me and joined the group.

The ginger studied me for a second and without looking away from me, asked, "What's the deal?" He was obviously talking to my captors. "What's this goody-two shoe doing here?" He gestured at me.

The boy with the dirty blonde hair and dragon tattoo that took me said, "We found her walking on the railroad tracks. We didn't know what you would want us to do, so we took her back here."

The ginger walked closer to me. He said, "Look, kid. The railroad tracks all the way back to here is our territory. You already know that we're here so . . . you're with us now." He turned around. As he was walking back, he looked over his shoulder and said, "Oh, and stop wearing such goody-two shoe clothes. You're gonna get hurt that way."

The ginger got back to the group, turned towards me, and put his arm around a blonde girl with freckles and brown eyes who looked about sixteen. Then he turned to the boy with the brown hair on the bottom and blonde hair on the top who took me. "Blade, won't you get this nice girl some clothes?"

Blade went over to the rusted old truck and asked, "Hey, kid! What size are you?"

"Fourteen," I responded.

Blade opened the door to the truck and brought out a black leather jacket, a white shirt, and some black pants. He closed the door, then came back to the group and gave me the clothes.

The ginger turned to me and said, "You wear this now, kid."

"Okay," I said. I walked a little closer so that I was only about one foot away from the group.

The ginger gestured at himself. "By the way, I'm Talon, spelled with an O," I noticed that he had an enamel pin on the collar of his jacket that looked like the claw of an eagle or some kind of bird. I realized that it was in reference to his name. It was a talon.

The girl he had his arm around said, "I'm Hatchet." I noticed that she was wearing a ring on her finger that had little skulls all the way around it, and also a big black leather bracelet with silver metal spikes. Her enamel pin looked like a kind of axe. It was a hatchet.

Blade said, "I'm Tactical Blade, but you can call me Blade." His pin was a pocket knife.

The other boy that took me, the one with dirty blonde hair said, "My name is Mangle." His pin was a slightly bloodied fist.

An Asian boy with dark skin, dark brown eyes and black hair said, "I'm Crippler." His pin was a cane.

"Okay," I said.

A girl with blonde hair and blue eyes said, "I'm Electrical Line, but you can call me E.L." I noticed that she was wearing a piece of leather cord with a piece of uneven glass on it around her neck as a necklace.

"What's that?" I asked, pointing to it.

She looked down at it. "Oh that? That's a shard of glass from my first store robbery. I broke a window of a convenience store trying to steal some candy bars." Her pin I thought was the coolest: a lightning bolt.

A different girl with brown hair and brown eyes said, "My name is Narcissist." Her pin looked like an anime sparkle.

The last boy with light skin, black hair and brown eyes turned towards me and said, "My name is Klepto." I noticed that he had the same dragon tattoo on his neck as Mangle. His pin looked like a hand holding something - a chocolate bar.

I guess my face was kind of contorted because Blade asked, "What's wrong?"

"I'm just wondering how you come up with your names," I said.

Talon said, "Well, our nicknames are based on our actual names."

"Do you come up with your own names?" I asked.

"No," said everyone but Talon.

Talon said, "I pick the names, kid. I'm the only one who chose my own name."

"Why do you get to pick all the names?" I asked.

"Because I made this group, kid. That's why," he responded. "Now, what's your name, kid?"

"Lauren," I responded.

Talon thought for a little bit. "Your new name is Lore."

"Laur?" I asked, "As in L-A-U-R?"

"No," he said, "Lore as in L-O-R-E. Creepy stuff, gore," he suggested.

"Okay," I said, "Can I still listen to my music?" I asked.

"What kind of music do you listen to?"

"Katy Perry, Carly Rae Jepson, stuff like that."

"No," he said, "You can listen to music, but you're with us now. You have to listen to Metallica, Godsmack, and stuff like *that*." He looked at me. "Why are you such a goody-two shoe?"

I got offended. "Why are you such a ginger?"

Everybody but Talon said, "Ooooooh!"

Talon looked very offended. He stuck his jaw out. He took out his lollipop, which was now just a stick, and threw it on the ground. He walked up to me and I started regretting my decision to call him a ginger. He said, "Don't say that ever. Again. You're with us now, so you give us the respect we demand."

I found my courage again and glared at him. "Ditto."

He walked back to the group and gestured to me with his head. "Take Lore home."

Blade and Mangle came up to me again – only this time,

they didn't take me by the arms. They started walking me in the direction of the rusty truck.

"Wait a minute," I said, "Where are we going now?"

Talon said, "We've seen you walk home before. This is way closer to your house than the railroad tracks."

"Huh," I said, "This is a shortcut? Good to know."

"See you tomorrow, kid," said Talon.

"How do you know I'll see you tomorrow?" I asked.

He turned around to look at me over his shoulder. "I just do."

CHAPTER TWO

THE NEXT DAY I went to school – Evergreen High. I still had my clothes in my backpack from Talon and the rest of the group. I had looked on the back of the jacket and it read *The Black Cougars*. The letters were written in red caps and curved around a picture of a roaring black cougar.

I decided to bring it to school, but not wear it. I noticed that someone had put on an enamel pin on the collar of the jacket. The enamel pin was a drop of blood. I guessed that was in reference to my name – Lore.

I also noticed that it was a reversible jacket. The inside was white leather instead of black and it read *The White Rabbits* in light pink curved around a cutesy picture of a bunny rabbit.

I was very confused by this. On that side, my enamel pin had also become a heart pin. I decided to let it go.

When I got to school, I saw a girl wearing a yellow shirt, a floral pattern skirt, and some red dress shoes. She had long blonde hair, freckles, blue glasses, and brown eyes. She was wearing a white leather jacket.

I recognized her, but I couldn't figure out from where. Then she brought her hand up to her face to move her hair behind her ear and I noticed she was wearing a skull ring. I realized where I'd seen her from.

"Hatchet!" I called. I waved at her.

Nobody seemed to pay attention to us.

Her face turned white and she quickly ran over to me.

"Hi, Hatchet!" I said.

"Ssshhhh!" she said, and she covered my mouth. She slowly lowered her hand.

"Why do we need to be quiet?" I whispered.

She said, "The Black Cougars are severely outlawed. Talon's already been to juvi three times because of it."

"Talon's been to juvi three times?" I asked.

"Just because of that," she said, "He's been to juvi plenty of other times."

"Oh," I said, "Okay."

"That's why our jackets are reversible," said Hatchet, "To keep everyone from going to juvi again."

"How many times has everyone gone to juvi?" I asked.

"It doesn't matter," she said. "You just can't yell out our Black Cougar names."

I looked at her clothes. "This is how I dressed yesterday.

Why are you teasing me about being a goody-two shoe when you have to dress up the same way?"

"You think I want to dress like this?" she pulled up part of her skirt, and then threw it back down. "I hate skirts! I don't like these clothes. I would rather be wearing a white t-shirt and black jeans. I hate hiding The Black Cougars. Once school is over, I'm taking all of this stuff off. I have my clothes in my backpack."

"So I can wear my jacket?" I asked.

"Of course," she said, "Just wear it inside out."

"I'm glad I chose not to wear it to school," I said.

"Yeah," she said, "That would have been an issue."

I took my backpack off and set it on the ground. I opened it up, turned my jacket inside out, and put it on. "Does everyone have a heart pin?" I asked.

"Just the girls," said Hatchet, "The guys have stars."

"Okay," I said.

Just then, the bell rang.

"What do you have next?" she asked.

"P.E.," I responded.

"Me too," she said, "With Mr. Daviar?"

"Yeah," I said.

"Okay. Let's go," Together we walked to Mr. Daviar's P.E. class.

When I got there, I realized that Talon was also in our

class. He was wearing his P.E. clothes. He had removed his earring, but he was again eating a round green lollipop. His eye was also uncovered, his hair behind his ear.

"Why do you like those so much?" I asked and pointed to his lollipop stick.

"I just like the green ones," Talon replied.

"Okay! Everybody be quiet so I can do roll," said the teacher. He started taking roll, looking up to see if the kid was there or not, occasionally checking off a kid who was absent.

"Hey, guys!" E.L. came over and sat down next to me. "Wow, I got here just in time I guess."

A little while later, Mr. Daviar finished the roll. Hatchet, Talan, E.L., and I were walking to the dirt track.

Apparently Talon had finished his lollipop because as was walking, he spit out his lollipop stick and put his arm around Electrical Line.

"So Lore," he said. "Do you like being a Black Cougar so far?" I noticed he made his voice a little quieter when he said, "Black Cougar".

"I think it's good," I said. "I have a question."

"What?" he asked.

"Who the heck are you dating?"

Talon made a contorted face at me. "What do you mean?"

"When I first met you, you put your arm around Hatchet, but now you're putting your arm around Electrical Line," I said. "So who the heck are you dating?"

"I'm not dating anyone," replied Talon. "I just do that because we're friends. If you notice, when you're around us," he turned to Hatchet, "Hatchet will put her arm around Crippler and Blade all the time."

His eyes went wide. "If you ask me," his voice turned loud but whispery, "she's dating both of them."

"Oh shut up!" said Hatchet. She slapped him in the arm and Talon started laughing.

Talon's face looked kind and gentle when he was laughing, but I knew that's not how he was.

After P.E., everyone met up in the lunch room outside and we ate our snack together for recess. Hatchet and Talon were murmuring about something that involved a party, two girls, and the police. I decided to let it go.

"So," I said. "What are we planning to do after school?"

Blade turned to me and said, "Well, tonight we are just going to go to the clearing and talk around the fire. We don't usually really have anything planned."

"Okay," I said. "Sounds like fun!"

We started laughing.

Talon asked me, "What class do you have next?"

"Math with Mr. Harrison," I replied.

He thought for a little bit. "Oh," he said, "Crippler and Tactical Blade are in that class."

"Okay," I said. Just then, the bell rang for recess to end.

When I got to math class, Crippler was standing there wearing a dark blue t-shirt that said *I completed Anderson Community Church VBS!* The text was above a picture of a cartoon man wearing the same shirt doing a thumbs-up. Crippler was also wearing denim jeans and glasses with the attachment that wraps around your head.

"So this is what you wear at school?" I asked.

He turned around. His face lit up. "Lore!" he said. "Good to see you." He gestured at the door to the classroom. "You in this class, too?"

"Yeah," I said.

"Lore!" said a voice behind me. I turned around to see Blade wearing a black and gray tie-dye t-shirt with khaki shorts and tennis shoes. He was still wearing his black bandana around his forehead.

"Hi," I said.

Blade put his arm around me, which I now understood didn't mean anything. "So, kid. How do you like being a Black Cougar so far?"

"It's good," I said. "I really like the clothes we wear."

"Me, too," said Blade. He pulled out his shirt and looked at it. "I don't like wearing this stuff."

"That seems to be the main consensus," I said. Just then, a cold breeze hit. Everyone rubbed their arms.

Blade shivered. "Why did it just get cold all of a sudden?"

I was already wearing my leather jacket, so I was fine, but

Blade and Crippler both had to pull out their jackets and put them on. Just then, Mr. Harrison came outside and said, "All right! Everybody come in!"

We walked into the classroom and I sat down in between Blade and Crippler. The teacher walked to the front of the room and picked up his list. He started doing roll the same way Mr. Daviar did.

Crippler leaned in to me and pointed at a girl towards the middle front of about fifteen with short blonde hair, blue eyes, and glasses. "That's Cramer. She's one of our moles who tell us information about other groups in this area. Same thing with Thompson," he pointed to another girl of about fifteen with brown hair and brown eyes, "and Taylor." He pointed to a boy of about sixteen with short blonde hair, blue eyes, and blue glasses.

Blade leaned in to me and pointed at a girl of about sixteen in the middle of the classroom with short brown hair pulled back in a ponytail and brown eyes. "That's Flower. She used to be a Black Cougar, but she left. She started a group called the Anti-Cougars. They have group jackets and everything."

Just then, as if on cue, Flower got up and turned around, revealing the back of her pink leather jacket. It said *The Anti-Cougars* in big black writing curving around the same cougar on the back of our jackets, but with a big red circle with a line through it over the cougar. She turned around and started walking toward us. Blade stayed in the same position and just followed her with his eyes.

"Did you see her enamel pin?" he asked.

Flower finished sharpening her pencil and started walking away. Just as she walked past us, I saw her enamel pin. Instead of a blood drop like me or a pocket knife like Blade, she had a red circle with a line through it, like the one on the cougar on the back of her jacket.

Crippler leaned in close to me and pointed to another girl of about fifteen who was wearing the same thing Flower was. He said, "Same deal with Peace there. She used to be a Black Cougar, but she left with Flower. They literally left together at the same time. Apparently, they're working together to put all of us in juvi again. The police have already caught us once. We were in juvi for a month. It was horrible in there. There were tons of juvenile delinquents, ages ranging all over. There were so many little kids that had done bad things, we couldn't believe it. We felt so bad for them. Then there was us, eight teenagers almost ready for real jail, dressed like 1950's greasers, surrounded by hardcore-looking ten and twelve-year olds."

Blade said, "We've all been to juvi for being associated with the Black Cougars once. That's because the first and third time, Talon took the blame for it. He said, 'Take me. I'm the leader. I formed this group.' Then they grabbed him by the arms and put him in juvi. He just got out two months ago."

Crippler said, "Talon's a month away from being eighteen, though. If he gets apprehended again, he'll go to real jail. The Slammer. The Big House." He looked up at the ceiling and made a confused face, then looked at me again. "People call jail The Big House, right?"

Blade said, "The point is, we can't get caught again."

"Hey!" said Mr. Harrison. "Are you three paying attention?" he gestured at us.

Blade rolled his eyes at me, and then turned to Mr. Harrison. "Yes, sir."

Crippler looked at me. "I can't wait 'til the end of school."

CHAPTER THREE

AFTER THE REST OF school went by, the last bell finally rang for us to go home. I excitedly pushed my way through the crowds of people to get to the bathroom to change my clothes.

After I finished getting changed, I put my jacket back on and texted my mom: *Can I hang out with some friends for a couple hours after school?* She responded with: *Sure. Be sure to be home by dinnertime: 6:30.* I replied with: *Okay.*

I put my phone in my backpack and ran outside to meet up with the rest of The Black Cougars.

Blade had his arm around Hatchet, Talon's arm around E.L.

"Took you long enough," said Klepto.

"Sorry," I said. "I had to text my mom to see if I could hang out with you guys after school. Don't worry – I didn't mention The Black Cougars at all."

"Good," said Mangle.

"Are you two brothers?" I asked Mangle, gesturing to him and Klepto.

Klepto look surprised. "Yeah. How'd you know?"

"I noticed you two have the same tattoo in the same place," I said. "I just assumed you got them at the same time."

Klepto put his arm around me. "Good perception, kid."

Mangle put his arm around Narcissist. "Let's go," he said.

Crippler looked around, but there were no more people to put his arm around. I noticed that Crippler had taken off his glasses. He must've put in contacts. Everybody watched him go around in circles. Blade started singing "All By Myself," and everyone started laughing.

Crippler glared at him. "Ha ha. Very funny." He turned to Mangle. "You're right. Let's go."

Everyone walked to the car and got in. Talon drove, Hatchet rode shotgun and we took off.

When we arrived at the clearing Blade and Mangle brought me to the night I joined The Black Cougars, Talon reached into his jacket pocket and brought out a pack of matches. He lit one and started another fire in the trash can. He then put the pack of matches back in his pocket and zipped it up.

"Do you just randomly carry around a pack of matches in your pocket?" I asked.

"Yeah," he said. "Is that wrong?"

I thought about it. "I'm not exactly sure. It is weird, though."

We gathered around the trash can because it was a little colder than it had been before that night. We were talking when all of a sudden, we heard rustling in the bushes. We turned our attention to the bush. The bushes around us started rustling, also. Everyone formed a protective circle around me.

Talon, Hatchet, (who had also taken off her glasses and put in contacts), Blade, and E.L. all pulled out pocket knives.

I whispered, "So are you guys, like, complete greasers from the 1950's or what?"

"Shut up," said Talon, "We might be saving your life."

All of a sudden, there was a deep laugh that almost sounded evil. Talon groaned and said, "Switchblade, just come out." Talon almost sounded relieved that he knew the people in the bushes, yet he didn't put away the pocket knife.

A boy around seventeen with black hair, olive skin, and brown eyes came out from the bushes. He was wearing the same thing we were wearing, but instead of black jackets and jeans, he was wearing a red leather jacket and red jeans. A bunch of other people wearing the same thing came out from the other bushes. "Hello, Talon. Nice to see you again." He was also holding a pocket knife.

Talon said, "Switchblade, why are you here?"

The person he must have been referring to, the seventeen

year old boy, studied the blade of his knife and said, "Call me Skull, Talon."

Another boy of about fifteen with pale skin, brown eyes, and brown hair came out from one of the bushes.

The first boy said, "I want you to meet one of my newest recruits and next in line to be leader of The Lions." He gestured to the second boy. "This is AR-15."

"How'd you come up with that name?" asked Talon.

The second boy said, "My real name is Arnold Ronson and I'm fifteen years old." He spread his arms. "AR-15."

The first boy brought down the knife and looked evilly up at Talon. "It's been a while since I've seen you around." He gestured at me. "What, did you pick up another kid at the railroad tracks?"

"Get out of here, Switchblade," warned Talon. "You know why we kicked you out. You weren't a Black Cougar. You didn't belong with us."

The boy looked at me and said, "Don't trust Talon, kid. He's full of lies and unfulfilled promises." He glared up at Talon. "He'll kick you to the curb, just like me."

I looked up at Talon. "Talon, what's he talking about?"

"Nothing," said Talon, keeping his eyes on the boy. "He's lying. Don't listen to him."

"The only one who ever lied was you," said the boy.

"I never lied to you, Switchblade."

"My name is Skull!" yelled the boy. He ran at Talon

with the knife and Talon caught his arm just before the boy cut him.

"Go!" Talon yelled at the others. "Protect Lore!"

"Oh, so you gave your new little recruit a new name too, eh?" the boy named Skull ripped his arm from Talon's grasp and went into a sideways somersault. He came up on one knee with the blade in his hand. He had an evil smile on his face as he looked at Talon.

Talon turned to The Black Cougars. "Go, now! Protect Lore!" He turned back to Skull just in time for Skull to run up to him again with the knife as they went into the same pose as when the Black Cougars were in the protective circle. Talon's hair went quickly forward and backward against his face when Skull slammed up against him. Talon and Skull were both bearing their teeth.

Skull turned his head towards the bushes and yelled, "Lions! Go!"

The other people wearing red greaser outfits charged at the rest of The Black Cougars. All the other Black Cougars reached into their pockets and pulled out their pocket knives. They all started fighting, trying to keep the blades away from themselves.

There was one Lion left. He looked about sixteen. He was looking around wildly. He locked eyes with me and ran towards me.

Oh boy, I thought, *here we go.* I yelled and charged at him.

CHAPTER FOUR

I SLAMMED INTO THE BOY with all my force. He stumbled backward, and then ran at me again. I stuck out my arms and we slammed into each other, pushing each other's shoulders.

I managed to slip out of his grasp by pushing my head under his arm and coming back up with my fists up.

I was relieved that he didn't have a knife, either. Otherwise, I probably would've lost many times. I swung my fist at him, but he ducked. He came up and swung his fist at me, but I reacted too late.

His fist made contact with my face and my face filled with pain. It was the first time I had ever been punched. I yelled in pain, then got hold of myself and put my fists up again.

I swung at him a second time, and I barely missed him. He swung at me, but this time, I was anticipating it. I leaned backward just in time to see his hand going over my face.

I punched at him again, only this time, I punched straight forward and nailed him in the nose. He stumbled backward, bent over, covering his nose. He stopped, looked at his hand, and ran at me again, this time with a bloody nose.

I didn't run into him again, though. I waited until he was in range, and then stuck out my fist again so his nose ran right into my fist.

The second time he got up he ducked under my hand and took a swing at my stomach. I jumped backward just in time, and then stood up and punched him, once again, in the nose.

I punched him over and over again until his legs were wobbly and his eyelids were droopy. He stumbled backward a little bit, then his eyes rolled up in the back of his head and he fell backwards onto the ground.

Narcissist looked over her shoulder for a second to see me standing over an unconscious Lion on the ground. She looked up at me. "Good job, kid." She turned her attention back to her opponent and head-slammed him. He fell on the ground backward, unconscious. Then she got protectively in front of me. "You're lucky, kid. You got a young Lion, so he was easier to take. If you had gotten one of the Lions that we're fighting, I don't know if you would've been able to take him."

Skull, who was still fighting Talon, looked over to see two Lions lying on the ground, knocked out cold, and Narcissist and I standing next to them. "Lions!" he called out. "Come on!"

Everyone broke free of their Black Cougar's grasp and retreated with Skull. One of the Lions on the ground woke up just in time to see everyone else retreating. He jumped up, stumbled a little bit (probably because of how dizzy he was), grabbed his head, shook his head, and ran after the rest of the group.

From far away, we heard Skull's voice shout out, "This isn't over, Black Cougars!"

Everyone sighed in relief and exhaustion. We gathered around the second still unconscious Lion that Narcissist had knocked out. He groaned and opened his eyes to see nine Black Cougars standing over him. His eyes went wide open and he scrambled backward a little bit.

Talon said, "The rest of your group left. You better join them."

The Lion jumped up and looked around.

Talon called out, "They went that way," he pointed to where the Lions had left.

The Lion ran in that direction yelling, "Guys, wait for me!"

Everybody laughed weakly as we started walking towards the rusty truck. Talon had a bad limp and Hatchet had to help him over to the truck. We sat down on the hood. Hatchet carefully made sure Talon could sit on the hood, then let him go and sat down on the hood herself.

Talon, E.L, and Mangle all had black eyes. Talon probably got the worst of it. He spit, and a tooth came out. His eyes went wide. "I'm really hoping that wasn't an adult tooth."

Everybody started laughing. Blade and Mangle stopped and both grabbed their sides.

Talon looked at everyone. "I'm serious! My dad will kill me if I lose another tooth." He felt around in his mouth, and then breathed a big sigh of relief. "It's okay, guys. This is actually good. I was going to get that tooth pulled out because it was stuck and the adult tooth couldn't come in."

Everybody started laughing. Talon leaned back onto the windshield and put his hands behind his head. Everyone else did the same. We were silent for a little while, just looking up at the stars.

Then Talon said, "So, same time next week?"

Everybody started laughing.

"Well," I said. "I have to get going. My mom told me I have to be home by 6:30."

"Okay," everyone said.

"Hey, wait," said Talon. He sat up and reached into his pocket. He pulled out an extra pocket knife and gave it to me. "For protection," he said.

I looked at it. The handle was black. On it, carved in red letters, it said *The Black Cougars*.

"Wow," I said. I looked up at Talon and smiled. "Thanks."

I hugged everyone as we said bye. Everyone went off in different directions, and I went home to have dinner with my family.

CHAPTER FIVE

THE NEXT DAY, I arrived at school. Hatchet and Crippler were wearing glasses again, and everyone was wearing "goody-two shoe clothes" again. Blade was still wearing his black bandana around his forehead. I didn't know what the deal was with Tactical Blade and that bandana. We were all wearing our jackets inside out again, also.

Talon came a little later because he still had the bad limp. E.L. and he came up to us. E.L. had to support Talon because his limp was so bad he couldn't walk on his own. He still had a black eye, along with Mangle and E.L., although theirs didn't look as bad.

"Why do we have to wear goody-two shoe clothes?" I asked. "Why can't the girls just wear t-shirts and jeans?"

Hatchet slapped her forehead. "Dag nab bit! Why didn't *we* think of that?" She turned to Talon.

He grinned and shrugged his shoulders. "I thought it was funnier watching you squirm around in a skirt."

Narcissist, who was also wearing a skirt, said, "Oh, bite me!" and slapped Talon on the shoulder, who of course, started laughing hysterically.

The first bell rang to start school. "Well," Blade said, "time for our first class."

E.L. said, "Who has Talon in their first class?" Blade and Narcissist raised their hands.

"Narcissist," said Talon. "Come over here."

Narcissist walked over and E.L. and her traded places supporting Talon.

"Hey!" said Blade. "Why didn't you call me over?"

Talon looked at Blade. "Because I know she's taller and stronger than you."

Everybody said, "Ooooooooh!" and they started laughing. Then we all said bye to each other, and everybody in groups walked in different directions.

After first class was over, we all met up again so that someone could switch places with Narcissist supporting Talon.

"Who has their second class with Talon?" Narcissist asked. Hatchet, Electrical Line, and I raised our hands.

E.L. said, "I helped him all the way to school this morning."

Hatchet said, "Fine. I'll do it."

"Hey!" I said. "Why don't you let me try?"

Hatchet looked at me. "He's pretty heavy."

I spread my arms. "I'm pretty strong."

Hatchet studied me for a second, and then said, "Alright. Fine. But don't say I didn't warn you." She stepped aside.

I walked over to Talon and traded places with Narcissist. We started walking to the next class. As soon as Narcissist let go, I realized just how hurt Talon was. He was putting a good three fourths of his body weight on me, and he was still limping.

"Talon," I said, "how badly did you hurt yourself?"

"I have no idea," he said. "It can't be any better than the last time we fought with Switchblade, though."

"By the way," I said. "What did Skull or Switchblade or whatever his name is mean when he said, 'You lied'?"

Talon grunted, which I guessed was as close as he could get to a sigh. "A few years ago, we found Switchblade by the railroad tracks, so we picked him up. It was basically the same scenario as you. We pick him up, we make him join The Black Cougars, we give him a name, and we give him the clothes. I promised I would always protect him. A few weeks after our first robbery with Switchblade, he became too violent. He started turning on fellow Cougars for no reason, picking fights with them, threatening them with his own pocket knife that we gave him." Talon shook his head. "He just became too dangerous. We had to kick him out of the group. He was endangering our lives. A short while afterwards, he joined The Lions, which is a group that is even more illegal than us. They're more dangerous, they break into stores for the valuable items, not just for food."

Talon shifted his weight, and then kept limping along. "A little while after he joined The Lions, he came after The Black Cougars. He had become the leader of The Lions. They had started following him." Talon shook his head. "I'm just glad he's not in The Black Cougars anymore. A lot of people could've gotten hurt if we had kept him. He belongs in The Lions. They're the most brutal group I know."

We arrived at the boys' locker room.

"You can walk inside?" I asked. "Or do I need to put on a blindfold?"

Talon started laughing. "I think I'm good. It'll just be painful." He took his arm off of me and immediately winced. He grunted. "Well, see you in a couple minutes." He started towards the locker room, barely putting any weight on his leg. He would walk with one leg, and then barely touch the ground with his other one. It was painful to watch.

I made sure he made it into the locker room, then ran over to the girls' locker room and got changed as quickly as I could.

A couple minutes later, I ran over to the boys' locker room

to see Talon limping out. I ran over and put my arm under him. His face immediately became less pained.

"Thanks," he said. "That helps a lot. Hatchet had to walk me home last night."

"No problem," I said.

We walked over to the bleachers.

Mr. Daviar did what he had done the time before. He just checked to see if everyone was there, then he said, "Okay, kids! Today, we are going to be doing the mile."

Talon just laughed and leaned back, putting his hands behind his head. "Looks like I get to skip out on the mile!"

E.L., Hatchet, and I groaned.

Hatchet said, "*We* still have to do the mile. Stop teasing us."

"Whoa, whoa, whoa," said Talon. "I get beat up so bad I can't walk and you're jealous because I get to skip out on *the mile*?"

"Oh please," said E.L. "You can walk."

"Not without assistance!" he said. "I literally have to have someone holding one side of my body up just so that I can walk properly!"

Hatchet said, "Fair point."

After Mr. Daviar finished roll call, he made everyone walk down to the track.

Hatchet said, "I can take him now."

"Okay," I said.

Hatchet helped Talon up, and then Talon put his arm

around her so she could support him. They walked down to the track like that.

When we got to the track, Mr. Daviar said, "What's wrong with *you?*"

Talon's face went pale (except for his black eye, of course). I knew what he was thinking. He couldn't just say, *I got beat up in a fight.* We would have to improvise.

"He fell down the stairs!" I said.

Talon looked at me like, *Thank you.*

"Yeah," he said. "I was just walking and I looked down at my watch to see what time it was, and so I accidently kept walking and fell down the stairs."

Mr. Daviar grunted. "I guess that makes sense. You can skip out on the mile. But you have to stand here and put the dots on people's arm so we know how many laps they've done."

"Okay," he said. Hatchet helped him over to where he was supposed to stand, then let go and held out her arms as if trying to balance a fragile object.

Talon could stand, but not very well. He looked like he was about to fall over because he was leaning so much on his other leg, his hurt leg almost wasn't even touching the ground.

"You sure you don't need a chair, kid?" asked Mr. Daviar.

"No," replied Talon. "I'm fine."

"Okay," said Mr. Daviar. He turned to us. "Listen! Four

laps around this track is one mile! You will get four dots on your arm to show that you have done all four laps! If you don't, you'll have to run it again next Tuesday!"

He blew his whistle, and we started running.

After P.E., we all met up again. I walked Talon back to the locker rooms and the place where we met up.

"Okay," I said. "Who wants to take Talon to the lunch room for recess?"

Nobody raised their hands.

"Oh come on!" I said. "Somebody has to do it."

After a little while, Klepto groaned and said, "Fine. I guess I'll do it." Klepto walked over and traded places with me supporting Talon. We walked to the lunch room to have recess.

During recess, we didn't talk very much. A couple people came over and asked Talon what happened to his leg, and he told everybody the same thing he told Mr. Daviar in P.E.

"I fell down the stairs," he said casually, like it happened every day.

That was about as much talking we got in during recess.

After recess, I decided to carry Talon again, since Klepto didn't want to and neither did anyone else.

We got to where we met up after our class and I said, "So, who has Talon in their next class?"

Mangle was the only one who raised his hand.

"Okay," I said. "I guess that's settled, then."

Mangle came over and traded spots with me.

"Well," said Mangle. "See you next period."

Everybody turned around and walked in groups in different directions.

CHAPTER SIX

B LADE, CRIPPLER, AND I walked to Mr. Harrison's math class.

"So," said Blade "is Talon heavy?"

"Yeah," I said. "But I could carry him, though."

Crippler asked, "How much body weight was he putting on you?"

"A good three fourths of his body weight." I responded. "He's hurt pretty bad."

"Wow," said Blade. "Three fourths? That *is* bad."

We walked into class and the teacher took roll.

"Hey, Blade?" I said.

"Yeah?"

I said, "Why do you wear that bandana around your forehead all the time?"

He looked as if he were coming up with an excuse. "I just really like it, okay?"

"Alllriiight," I said. He had sounded suspicious.

"Hey, Lore," said Crippler. "We're going to go to the clearing tonight to look at the stars. Want to come? Everybody's going to be there!"

"I'll have to check with my parents," I said. "But sure! It sounds fun."

"Oh it is!" said Blade. "We're going to roast marshmallows and make s'mores over the fire. It's so fun! We do it every year. You're lucky we didn't find you too late or you would've missed it."

Crippler said, "It's called 'The Black Cougars Celebration Party'. It's called that because all the Black Cougars come every year! Sure there are only around a dozen of us, but still!"

"Okay!" I said. "I'll be sure to check."

Blade said, "You don't want to miss it."

Crippler said, "When Peace and Flower were still Black Cougars, we invited them to the party and they said that they had a really good time. It was fun."

"Okay!" Mr. Harrison said. "It's time to start math! Who's excited?"

Everyone groaned.

Crippler rolled his eyes and turned to me. "Trust me. It's *way* better that this."

After math, we met up again. Mangle walked with Talon

to where we met up and said, "Okay, who has Talon in their next class?"

Nobody raised their hand.

"Uh oh," said Talon.

"Who do you have next, Talon?" said E.L.

"I have Mrs. Alfonzo."

"Okay," she said. "Who has Mr. Robinson? He's the class right next to Mrs. Alfonzo."

Nobody raised their hand.

"Who has Ms. Wallybean? She's to the right of Mrs. Alfonzo."

Klepto, Crippler, and Hatchet all raised their hands.

Klepto and Hatchet turned to Crippler and Hatchet said, "Crippler, I don't think you've carried Talon at all today." She gestured her head towards Talon. "I think it's your turn."

Crippler reluctantly said, "Okay," and he traded places with Mangle.

As soon as Mangle let go, Crippler grunted. He was obviously struggling. "Why are you so heavy?" he said. To be fair, Crippler was only about late fifteen, early sixteen and he was a little bit skinny. Talon was late seventeen and pretty fit, so Talon had a lot more muscle mass and was a lot heavier than Crippler was.

Talon turned slowly to Crippler and looked at him with just utter disbelief. "Are you sure you'll be able to carry me?"

"Yeah," grunted Crippler, trying to breathe steadily. "It'll just be kind of hard."

Talon just shook his head. "Okay."

Crippler, who had slowly started sinking to the ground, said, "Start walking, start walking!"

Everyone started laughing. The bell rang and everyone said bye to each other. For a few classes after that, everyone called him Crippled instead of Crippler.

After school was over, we changed in the bathrooms and packed into the car again, but this time Hatchet was driving because everyone was worried about Talon's foot not being able to step on the peddles, despite Talon's denials. Talon still rode shotgun, though.

When we got out of car, Blade got out of the car before Talon to support him because we decided that it was his turn to help Talon. Blade looked like an actual 1950's greaser with his black leather jacket, his white t-shirt, his black jeans, and his black bandana around his forehead.

We walked to the clearing and Blade set down Talon on the hood of the rusty truck so that he could rest his leg while everyone else stood around the trash can.

Blade went out into the bushes for a little while. He didn't tell us why, though. A few minutes later, Blade came back with a bunch of wrapped sandwiches.

"Guys!" he said. "Look what I got!"

Everyone started walking over.

E.L. said, "Yeah!"

Hatchet said, "I'm starving!"

I just stood there. "Where did you get those?" I asked.

Blade took a big bite out of one of the sandwiches. "A small restaurant."

I asked, "Did you *steal* those?"

"Yeah," he said. "What's the problem?"

"Why would you do that?" I asked.

He looked like a deer caught in headlights. "We need to eat somehow."

"What do you mean?" I asked. "Don't your guys' parents feed you at home?"

Talon said, "Yeah, I've been meaning to talk to you about that."

"About what?" I asked.

"About parents," he responded.

"What about parents?" I asked.

Talon sighed. "Not everybody has parents, you know. In fact, most of the people in this group have only one parent." He gestured at himself. "I only have a dad."

Crippler said, "Me, too.

Narcissist said, "Me, too."

E.L. said, "I only have a mom."

Blade said, "I don't have any parents."

Hatchet turned to me and said, "See, Lore? Mangle,

Klepto, you, and I are the only ones who have both of our parents. Sometimes, for the people that only have one parent, it's hard for them, so they steal to eat."

"Okay," I said. "Sorry."

Blade said, "Hey, no hard feelings." He held out a sandwich to me. "Want some?"

CHAPTER SEVEN

AFTER WE FINISHED OUR sandwiches (which were not bad, by the way), three people showed up.

Talon's face lit up. "Hey, guys! Glad you could make it!"

There was a girl of about fifteen with brown hair and brown eyes. I recognized her from school. It was Thompson, one of the moles. She obviously had the correct attire for The Black Cougars.

Later, I found out that the moles were called by their last names.

There was another girl of about fifteen with long blonde hair, and blue eyes. It was Cramer, another one of the moles. She had taken off her glasses and put in contacts, and she was also wearing Black Cougar clothes.

The last person to show up was a boy of about sixteen with short blonde hair, blue eyes, and blue glasses. It was Taylor, the last mole. He had also dressed out in Black Cougar attire.

"Hi," I said. "Why are you still wearing your glasses?"

"I don't like contacts," he said. "They irritate my eyes."

"Oh," I said. "Okay."

Everybody laid on the rusted truck again and looked up and watched the stars. We could see Orion, and The Big Dipper, and The Milky Way. It looked so cool.

A little while after that, someone pulled out a bag of marshmallows from the truck and a few cleaned up sticks. They also brought out graham crackers and Hershey's chocolate bars.

We were sitting around the fire roasting marshmallows, when we heard the bushes rustling.

Talon rolled his eyes. "Again, Switchblade?"

Blade, E.L., and Hatchet all pulled out their pocket knives.

But something told me this wasn't Switchblade.

A girl of about sixteen came out of the bushes. She had short brown hair pulled back in a ponytail, brown eyes, and she was wearing a light pink leather jacket with jeans and a floral pattern shirt with a white background.

Talon's face went contorted. "What? Why are *you* here?"

The girl looked at Talon and said, "Why do you think I'm here, Talon?" She turned to Hatchet. "Or maybe I should be asking you, Hatchet."

Another girl came out of the bushes. She had short brown hair, brown eyes, and was wearing a light pink leather jacket with jeans and a white blouse.

"We're here to put you in jail," the second girl said.

Blade groaned. "Oh, come on! It's The Black Cougar Celebration Party!"

"Yes," said the first girl. "We knew that. That's why we came. We knew all of you would be here."

Hatchet crossed her arms and shook her head. "Not cool, man."

Talon said, "Come on, Fall Out. You used to be a Black Cougar."

The first girl said, "Don't call me Fall Out. My name is Flower."

Talon turned to the second girl. "You too, Animal. Why are you trying to put us in jail when you used to *be* one of us?"

The second girl said, "My name is not Animal. It's Peace."

The first girl, Flower, said, "If you won't come voluntarily, I guess we'll have to take you by force." She ran up to Hatchet and they started fighting. Hatchet took a swing at Flower's head, but she ducked.

Flower tried to apprehend Hatchet, but Hatchet kept wiggling out of whatever position she was put in.

This went on for about fifteen minutes. Hatchet threw Flower to the ground. When Flower got up, I noticed she had dropped an old picture. They had moved away from it, so I swooped down and grabbed it.

It was a picture of a middle-aged woman with long brown

hair and brown eyes. She was wearing a light pink blouse and she was smiling. She was very pretty.

"Hey," I called. "What's this?"

Flower turned around. Her eyes went wide and her face went pale. "Give me that!" she shouted and she ran at me, but Blade apprehended her. She struggled to break free. "That's mine! Don't rip it!"

"What is it?" I asked.

"It's my mom," she said, still struggling. "She died when I was little, so I carry around a picture of her in my shoe. Give it back!"

"Okay!" I said. I handed it to her and she carefully put it back in her shoe.

Flower was breathing hard. She said, "Well, I guess it's time for Plan B."

Peace turned around and said, "Guys, they're over here!"

Talon turned toward us and said, "Run!" He got off of the truck and started going as quickly as his legs would take him.

Everyone else and I jumped into some bushes (away from Flower and Peace, of course).

A bunch of police jumped out of the bushes that Flower and Peace were in and started running towards Talon. They grabbed him, put him stomach-side-down on the rusty truck, and put handcuffs on him.

The one who put handcuffs on Talon turned around to rest of them. "We got the leader," he said. He turned back to

Talon. "We're not going to take your friends. We don't care about them. We just care about you."

Something about his tone told me he was lying. We stayed hidden in the bushes.

We all looked at Talon on the truck. He wasn't struggling to break free.

The police laughed. "You're too old for juvi now, boy. You get to go to *real* jail."

They laughed as they put Talon in the back of the police car that was cleverly hidden behind the bushes (I mean seriously! Where are all these bushes coming from?).

They drove off towards the police department. They had to do a one day registration for Talon, and then the next day they could put him in real jail.

The next day, all of The Black Cougars were silent throughout the whole school day. When school finished, we didn't change our clothes. We went to see Talon in the jailhouse.

We arrived at the jailhouse and walked in just in time to see Talon and the police officers. Talon was still wearing his Black Cougar outfit. Talon didn't look scared at all. If anything, he looked annoyed.

The officers had Talon's hands behind his back, even though he wasn't wearing handcuffs. They threw him into a cell and Talon stumbled a little bit, grabbing his leg and wincing after catching his balance. One of the big, nasty and mean-looking prisoners walked up to Talon, who was looking at him.

The prisoner was probably in his mid-30s. He was wearing an orange jumpsuit. He walked up to Talon and said in a very deep voice with a Brooklyn accent, "Hey, guys. It looks like we got some vintage 1950's greaser kid here." Then, with fake sympathy, his eyes went wide and he said, "Oh no! It looks like your leg's hurt. Do we need to get an ice pack for you?"

The other prisoners did a low, mean chuckle. Talon just rolled his eyes at the first prisoner, then turned around and looked out through the metal bars. He looked over his shoulder to see their reactions.

The first prisoner's eyes went wide and he backed up. "You're a Black Cougar!"

The other prisoners gasped. Talon just rolled eyes, turned his head back around, and leaned on where they connect the bars in the middle horizontally. His elbows were on the bar, and his forearms were sticking out of the cell.

We checked in with the security guard to see if it was okay if we could visit Talon. We walked up to Talon and said, "Hey, Talon."

Talon turned his head and spit on the ground.

"How is it here?" said Hatchet.

Talon said, "It's a little cold. The wall is damp; I don't know what that's about."

We started laughing.

The first prisoner in the back said to us, "Why are you hanging out with this kid?"

Talon turned around. "They're with me, okay?"

The prisoner seemed to get what that meant, because his face went pale.

Talon turned back around.

"What did that mean?" Hatchet asked.

Talon said, "I told him you were Black Cougars without the police knowing."

"Oh," said Hatchet. "Okay."

Talon said, "They won't tell me how long I'm here for. They just said, 'Long enough.'" Talon threw his hands up and made a face. "What am I supposed to do with that?"

We started laughing again.

Narcissist said, "Okay, Talon. We have to go."

Crippler said in an announcer voice, "Don't go away! We'll be right back after these messages!"

We all started laughing and Mangle said, "Okay! You know it's time to go when Crippler starts making announcer jokes." Mangle walked up to Talon, gently slapped him on the arm and said, "See you later, man."

Talon kind of moved his hand in a small wave. "See you later."

We all drove back to the schoolyard and changed our

clothes. We then drove to the clearing, and Hatchet took a pack of matches out of her pocket.

"Does everybody in The Black Cougars carry around a pack of matches?" I asked.

"No," said Hatchet. "Just Talon and I."

"Why is that?" I asked. "Why is it always just you and Talon that do or have special stuff?"

Hatchet said, "Well, Talon does because he is the leader, so he gets whatever he wants. I do because if something happens to Talon, then I would be the new leader, so I'm next in line."

"Oh," I said. "Okay. I guess that makes sense."

Hatchet started a fire in the trash can, then waved everyone else over to warm their hands around the fire.

"So," said Blade. "How long do you think Talon is going to be in jail?"

Narcissist shook her head. "I have no idea."

Everyone else agreed.

E.L. said, "He was usually in juvi for around two or three weeks. So probably a month."

Everybody groaned.

"Yeah," said Hatchet. "I don't like it either. I would rather have Talon as the leader, not me, but that's how it's going to be for probably a while."

We all just sat there and stared at the fire. Klepto said, "I'm really worried about Talon's leg. What if the other cell mates beat him up and make his leg worse?"

Mangle just looked at him. "You really think Talon is going to get beat up? Did you *see* how scared the prisoner looked? His face turned pale when he realized that Talon was a Black Cougar."

Klepto shrugged. "Good point."

Crippler said, "Yeah, I think he'll be just fine. And if he's not, we can just help him out again."

E.L. said, "On the plus side, we won't have to carry him around school for a while. His leg might actually heal up, depending on how long he's in there for."

"Why would they let Talon out if he's a Black Cougar?" I asked. "Don't they know he'll just go right back to being a Black Cougar?"

Hatchet said, "I think they know that, but I don't think they care. I think that after a while, they just don't want us in there anymore."

"Huh," I said. "Okay."

We all laid down on the truck and looked up at the stars.

After a little while, I said, "Why do we have group jackets and stuff if we are outlawed and have to hide it during school?"

Hatchet said, "We shouldn't be scared or ashamed of who we are, even if we're outlawed. The only reason we don't wear the jackets at school is because there's too many people. We tried wearing it once, but about four people called the cops on us. So we don't wear them to school anymore."

"Oh," I said. "Okay. I guess that makes sense."

Blade turned to me and said, "You sure do seem to say that a lot."

"Okay." I said. "Is that bad?"

"No," said Blade. "I was just making an observation."

We were silent for a little bit.

Then Electrical Line said, "Hey, Hatchet. Can we camp out here tonight?"

Hatchet thought about it, and then said, "That's actually a pretty good idea."

"What?" I said.

Narcissist sat up and said, "We always keep sleeping bags in the bed of the truck because we like to sleep out here sometimes. Everybody gets a sleeping bag and we sleep in the truck. Want to join us?"

"Sure!" I said. "Let me just check to see if it's okay first."

"Okay," Hatchet said from the bed of the truck. "Just hurry back."

I got off the truck and stepped away a few yards and pulled out my phone to text my mom: *Can I have a sleepover with my friends tonight?*

She took a little bit to respond. Then she said, *Sure. Love you.*

Thanks. I said and returned to the group.

Hatchet had pulled out sleeping bags for only about half the people there. Apparently, there were no Black Cougar-themed pajamas, so we had to sleep in our t-shirt and jeans.

"Why are there not enough sleeping bags?" I asked.

Hatchet said, "Well, winter is only a week away and it's getting colder, so we share sleeping bags. Usually, a boy and a girl sleep in one because the boy is bigger, so he keeps the girl warmer than if the two girls were to sleep side by side. Also, the boys get teased if they sleep side by side."

"Oh," I said. "Okay."

Hatchet and Mangle were sleeping by the foot pedals; Narcissist and Blade were sleeping on the driver and passenger seat, which was surprisingly big enough to hold both of them; and Klepto and E.L. were sleeping on the top of the truck (they had to be strapped down so they wouldn't fall off).

I got into one of the sleeping bags. It was in the bed of the truck. Crippler got into the bag also, and we turned so that our backs we together and we were facing away from each other. All the other Black Cougars did the same.

I only woke up once in the middle of the night. I was shivering because of how cold it was. I moved a little bit closer to Crippler, who had turned on his other side. He looked fine, but he had put his jacket back on. I got closer so that my back was barely touching him and I started to warm up. In a little bit, I fell asleep again.

When everyone woke up the next morning, it was cool and crisp outside. Blade looked at Narcissist and said, "Time to get the winter jackets out?"

"Definitely," Narcissist said.

Blade, still wearing his bandana, got up and opened up the driver side door of the truck. He pulled out big, poofy jackets that were the same as the leather jackets: reversible, names and group logos on both sides.

"Are these the winter jackets?" I asked.

"Yeah," said Hatchet.

"They look warm." I noted. I turned to everyone and said, "See you in a little bit!" I turned and started walking home to have breakfast.

After breakfast, I returned to the clearing. "Okay," I said. "My mom said it was okay if you guys drove me to school."

"Okay," said Hatchet. She turned to everyone else. "Should we have breakfast?"

"Yeah!" everyone said in unison.

"Okay," said Hatchet. She turned to Blade. "Blade, could you get the food out?"

"Sure," he said and walked to the truck.

"Wait," I said. "You guys have food? Why do you steal food if already have food?"

"We usually don't," explained Klepto. "Occasionally, we'll find a bunch of stuff to recycle, and then we get money from that and buy food. We don't like stealing if we don't have to."

"Oh," I said. "Alright, then."

"We can't get recyclables by rooting through trash," said Hatchet. "We tried once. The person called the cops on us."

"Okay," I said.

Blade came back with pre-cooked bacon, pancakes, and eggs.

"Wait, wait, wait," I said. "If you only occasionally get money for food, then how did you get all this expensive stuff?"

"We save up," said Mangle. "We usually try to get good breakfasts so that we're not just eating something we don't like."

"Wow," I said. "You sure are picky for people who can't afford food."

"Yeah," Klepto laughed. "Flower and Peace used to tease us about that, too."

"Okay, guys!" Hatchet yelled. "Come on over!"

Everyone but me grabbed two slices of bacon, one pancake, and one egg. They also grabbed a paper plate and started a fire in the trash can. They put their food on the paper plates and took turns heating their food up with the fire. Then they would sit down on the rusty truck and eat slowly, savoring the food.

After everyone was done, Blade pulled a gallon of milk out of the truck and paper cups. He poured everyone a glass, and then poured himself a glass. Everybody drank their milk, and then Blade pulled some clothes out of the truck. But these were regular clothes. He handed them out and everyone picked a different bush to change behind. I had already changed though, so I didn't need to change my clothes.

After everybody came out, Blade stretched and said, "Well, time to go visit Talon."

Everybody turned their jackets inside-out and got into the car, Hatchet driving and Blade riding shotgun.

When we arrived at the jailhouse, we walked in to see Talon lying on his back.

Hatchet saw him and ran up to him. "Oh my God, Talon are you okay?"

Talon groaned and moved a little bit, then looked up at us, squinting. "Oh hey, guys," he said.

Hatchet groaned. "Were you sleeping?"

"Yeah," said Talon. "Why?"

Hatchet sighed and said, "We thought you were hurt. Like, you got beat up or something."

"What?" Talon said. He stood up.

"By the way," said Klepto, "how's your leg?"

"It's good," said Talon. "It doesn't hurt as much as a few days ago."

"Good," said Mangle. "By the way, how long are you in for?"

"Two weeks," said Talon. "They said that because it's my first time in jail, so I could leave earlier than when I was in juvi." He leaned in close. "Personally, I could live here if I wanted to. I don't, but still."

We all started laughing.

Blade looked at his watch. "Hey, Talon. We have to go. Sorry, man."

Talon shrugged. "It's okay. I'll be right here when you come back."

Everyone said bye to him and we loaded up into the car to go to school.

When we got to school, the first bell had already rang, so we had to run to our classes.

I got there just as the teacher started taking roll.

"Ah," said Mrs. Sanders, my science teacher. She was obviously talking to me. "It's nice of you to join us today."

Everybody chuckled.

"Why were you late?" she asked. "You've never been late before."

I caught my breath, trying to think of an excuse. "I got stuck in traffic." I said.

Mrs. Sanders looked at me and said, "Alright, then. Go take a seat."

I sighed and grinned. I took my seat in the back of the class.

CHAPTER EIGHT

AFTER OUR FIRST CLASS, I met up with Hatchet and E.L. to go to our next class: P.E. with Mr. Daviar.

E.L. said, "Okay. What are we going to tell Mr. Daviar about Talon?"

I thought about it. "We could say he's at a doctor's appointment to check out his leg."

Hatchet shook her head. "Talon's not going to be at a doctor's appointment for two weeks."

"Hmm," I said, and I thought more.

Electrical Line's eyes went big and she snapped her fingers. "We can say that he's taking a trip with his family!"

My eyes went big. "Yes!" I said. "That's perfect!"

We arrived at the bleachers.

Mr. Daviar looked around. He was obviously checking to see if Talon was here or not.

I looked at E.L. and Hatchet like, *I got this.*

I leaned over to Hatchet and said, "What's Talon's real name?"

"Talan, spelled with an A," Hatchet whispered.

I just looked at her. "Really?" I said sarcastically. "His actual name is Talan?" I just laughed. "Real creative, there."

I raised my hand and said, "Talan isn't here."

"Do you know where he is?" asked Mr. Daviar.

"Yes," I said. "He is on a trip with his family."

"Okay," said Mr. Daviar. He checked Talon's name off and he went through the rest of the list.

After Mr. Daviar was done with roll call, he said that we were doing three laps, and then he sent us down to the track.

As we were walking, Hatchet said, "I'm worried about Talon. Who knows what will happen to him if he's in jail for two weeks."

"He doesn't seem very worried," I said. "He just looked annoyed."

Hatchet said, "He probably is. He's been to juvi, like, five times before, three for being a Black Cougar."

E.L. said, "Honestly, that's probably pretty bad. Imagine what'll happen when he tries out for a job interview."

Hatchet and E.L. looked at each other, and it almost looked like they were trying not to laugh. Then they started laughing really hard.

Hatchet wiped her eye and said, "Could you imagine Talon with a job?" she laughed hard. "Just imagine: Talon with his swooped over emo hair, wearing a McDonald's outfit, saying, 'May I take your order?'"

They laughed so hard, they almost fell over.

"What's so funny?" I asked.

Hatchet looked at me and said, "None of The Black Cougars have jobs."

"That's bad," I said.

E.L. shrugged. "Probably. But we usually just steal food to support ourselves. Nobody would let us have a job if they found out we were Black Cougars."

I looked at E.L. and said, "Maybe we should . . . disband The Black Cougars? So that we can get steady jobs?"

Hatchet just looked at me. "We can't just *disband* The Black Cougars. We're a family. We support each other, we protect each other, and we defend each other. We even give a home to Blade. Where would he go if we disband The Black Cougars?"

I shrugged. "He would probably go back to his family and have a good life with his parents."

E.L. shook her head. "Blade doesn't have any parents, remember? And, he's already been in social services. He said it was horrible. He kept running away because he knew that if he got in trouble, then his caretakers would get mad at him. He didn't want to let them down, but he also has mild kleptomania. He kept getting in trouble. Then he found us, so we're his family now. We can't leave him."

"Oh yeah," I said. "Good point. I forgot he didn't have any parents."

Hatchet said, "Many people often do. He never talks about wishing he had parents or anything. He doesn't seem depressed at all, and he doesn't seem mad like orphans usually do."

E.L. said, "Blade also doesn't like being called an orphan. He calls himself something long. What was it?" she turned to Hatchet.

Hatchet said, "He calls himself a 'parent-less child that has found another family.'"

"Yeah, that." E.L. said. "Why did he pick such a complicated term?"

Hatchet just chuckled and said, "*Actually* though."

We all started laughing.

Mr. Daviar said, "Alright! Today we are going to do three laps again. You have to get a time of eleven minutes to get a C, ten minutes to get a B, and nine minutes to get an A."

We all waited for Mr. Daviar to blow the whistle to start our three laps. He came down to the track, blew his whistle, and we took off running.

After our second class, we all met up for recess. Hatchet put her arm around Crippler and E.L. put her arm around Blade, though he had to bend down a little bit. Narcissist put her arm around Mangle, and I put my arm around Klepto.

"Well," said Klepto, "at least now we know how long Talon will be in jail."

"Yeah," said Narcissist. "That's good information to know because now we can tell the teachers how long he'll be gone."

"Yeah," Mangle agreed.

Hatchet said, "I wasn't really ready for Talon to go to jail. Well, I wasn't really ready to take over for him."

"Neither was anyone else," said Klepto dramatically.

Hatchet just said, "Wooooowww."

Everybody started laughing. We walked to the recess area and took out our food and started eating. Well, me and a few other people took out our food and shared it with the other Black Cougars.

Anyways, we sat there talking about what we would do when Talon got out of jail.

"We should camp out again," said Klepto.

"Yeah!" I said. "That's a really good idea."

"Oh," Mangle said, "so you liked the campout?"

"Yeah," I said. "It was so fun."

"Well then," said Hatchet, "it's settled. To celebrate Talon getting out of jail, we will all camp out again."

"Yes!" E.L. and Narcissist did a fist pump.

A few minutes later, the bell rang. Blade, Crippler, and I went together to Mr. Harrison's math class. We all put our arm around each other with me in the middle.

After school, we all met up but didn't change our clothes. We drove to the jailhouse to visit Talon.

When we arrived, Talon was leaning against the bars the way he was the day he was put in jail. He had his elbows on the center part and one of his forearms was sticking out of the cell. His other hand was on his chin, letting his head rest on his hand. The way his head was placed on his hand, it made his lips stick out a little bit so it looked like he was pouting.

Talon was now wearing an orange jumpsuit. Surprising, the look seemed to fit him. He was also still wearing his hair across his left eye and his earring. Somehow, he had found another green lollipop to eat.

We walked up and Talon said, "Hey, guys."

"Hi," said Hatchet. "How's it going?"

Talon looked at her sarcastically. "I'm in freaking jail."

"Good point, good point," said Hatchet.

Talon turned to me and said, "How are you doing, Lore?"

"Good," I said. "We just had a campout last night."

Talon said, "What?" he turned to Hatchet. "I missed Lore's first campout? Ah, man!" He turned and kicked a few little pebbles on the ground.

"It's okay," said Klepto. "We're going to have another campout to celebrate when you get out of here."

"Cool," said Talon. "I'm looking forward to it. I haven't been on a campout with you guys in, like, five months. It's going to be awesome!" He fist pumped.

Hatchet chuckled. "Well, we've got to get going."

"Okay," said Talon. "I can't wait to get out of jail!"

When we got back to the clearing, everyone changed their clothes. We got to put on our new winter jackets, which were very warm. Hatchet put on a black beanie with the Black Cougars logo on it. She also handed one out to everyone else.

With the beanie and the puffy jacket on, Hatchet looked like a teenage criminal (well, more of one anyway). There were parts of her hair that were laid on her shoulders and the rest of her hair was down her back. Now all she needed to be in a rap video were a couple rings on her fingers and a nose ring.

Hatchet went over to the trash can and started a fire. Everyone gathered around it and warmed their hands. Now, we actually *had* a reason to put a fire in the trash can. I guess before, we just used it kind of as a light or something we could talk around.

After a little while of silence, Blade said, "Do you think the prisoners will ever get over their fear of Talon?"

E.L. chuckled. "I sure hope not."

Narcissist said, "Yeah. That would be really bad. Did you see how much bigger and stronger they were?"

"Yeah," said Klepto. "They were huge compared to Talon!"

Mangle said, "I think I might have seen Talon go pale just a little bit when he first saw them. I know I sure did."

Crippler said, "Talon is really good at hiding his emotions. One time, he fell off the water tower near here and he didn't even scream. If anything, he sounded angry. He was just grunting a lot. I think he might've broken his leg and a couple of his ribs."

"Wow," said Mangle.

"I know, right?" said Crippler. "I was impressed."

"I would be," said Klepto. "I would probably pass out or scream or something."

"Me too," said Hatchet, Narcissist, Crippler, and Mangle. They all looked at each other and started laughing.

"Yeah," I said. "Me, too."

Hatchet said, "I would probably barf or something. I have a pretty weak stomach."

"Me, too," said Electrical Line.

We all laughed and sat around the fire for a while. Then, we all walked over and sat down on the truck, staring at the fire. E.L. put her arm around Crippler, and Blade put his arm around Narcissist.

Hatchet's eyes looked droopy. Her head kept bobbing. Then she almost fell off the truck.

"Come here," said Klepto and he waved her over.

Hatchet yawned and scooted closer to Klepto. He put his arm around her and she closed her eyes and fell asleep. Her head fell onto his shoulder.

"Well," said Mangle as he put his arm around me. "It looks

like we're camping out again." He jumped off the truck and walked around to the bed of the truck. He got in and pulled out the sleeping bags.

"Hey, Klepto," he said. "Where do you and Hatchet want to sleep?"

"How about we sleep on the ground this time?" said Klepto. "I don't think Hatchet's waking up, and I'm not lifting her body into the truck."

"Okay," said Mangle.

After Mangle had finished getting all of the sleeping bags out, Klepto took off Hatchet's jacket and carried her over to a sleeping bag. He gently set her down into one, and then got in next to her. They had their backs to each other.

Blade and Narcissist got into a bag, E.L. and Crippler got into a bag, and Mangle and I got into a bag. We all said goodnight quietly to each other and went to sleep.

CHAPTER NINE

THE NEXT MORNING, I woke up and about half of The Black Cougars were already awake, including Hatchet, who was getting out a frying pan and lighting a fire in the trash can.

"Hey," she said. "Did you sleep well?"

"Yeah," I said. "Did you?"

Hatchet chuckled. "Yeah, sorry about that. I've just been kind of stressed lately with Talon going to jail and all."

Blade sat up and yawned. "I think we all have."

Hatchet chuckled. "Does anybody want some pancakes? We still have some left from last time."

"I do!" yelled Blade, waking Narcissist and Klepto. He turned to them and said, "Sorry, guys."

"It's okay," said Klepto as he yawned. "I was already awake." Klepto stretched and got up with drooping eyelids.

Blade chuckled. "*Sure* you were."

Klepto said, "I was!" He stretched his back and groaned. "I'm tired."

"Yeah, me too," said Crippler, who was standing right by Hatchet, waiting for pancakes.

Hatchet turned to Crippler, who was looking over her shoulder at the pancakes being made. "Will you go sit down?" said Hatchet.

Crippler looked like he was surprised. "What? Why?" he asked.

"Because I told you to," said Hatchet, obviously annoyed.

"Okay," said Crippler reluctantly. He turned back to the sleeping bags still holding his plate, his head drooping.

Hatchet flipped a pancake. "Hey, Lore," she said, looking over her shoulder.

"Yeah?" I said.

Hatchet kept watching the pancakes. "I still have some footage of Crippler spazing out when we were in 7th grade." She flipped a pancake. "Wanna see?"

"No!" said Crippler. "Don't show her!"

"Why?" asked Hatchet.

"I look extremely weird in that!"

"You look extremely weird now."

Crippler thought about that for a moment. Then he raised his eyebrows, looked down and started shaking his finger at her saying, "True, true."

"Okay," Hatchet put a pancake on Crippler's, Blade's, and

her own plate, and then she opened up the driver side of the truck and got out a cell phone.

Hatchet got it all cued up, and then said, "Okay, guys. Come here."

Everybody gathered around and watched.

The video started with Crippler in a driveway. He was much younger, maybe twelve. The driveway had a white SUV in it, and behind that, a big bush.

Crippler was wearing a grayish zip-up jacket, and he had glasses on with the wrap-around fabric and denim jeans. He pressed something on his phone and fast music with a high-pitched voice in Japanese started playing.

Crippler started "dancing" by swinging his arms back and forth like a monkey might do. He stopped after a few seconds and stopped the music.

Without looking up from his phone, he said, "Hey, I memorized the English version."

He touched something on his phone, and then started spazing out, screaming what I thought to be lyrics. He was making movements that I didn't think could be humanly possible.

Crippler was spazing out while quote-on-quote singing, which I thought to be pretty impressive. He was making weird movements all around the driveway, screaming, "AND I WOULD LIKE TO FIND, A HAND LIKE YOURS TO TAKE IN MIINE AND MAKE ONE KISS. WE

COULD STOP TIME AND I'LL FLY HOME WITH YOU. TOMORROW'S FAR AWAY . . ."

After that, it became unrecognizable as real words. In the video, Crippler stopped and said, "Oh god," then collapsed in the driveway, smiling. The camera got closer so that it was right up next to Crippler's face, and Crippler said faintly, "All that spazing out . . ."

He chuckled, then looked over his shoulder and put his hand to his mouth and yelled, "I'M OKAY."

He sat up and a voice I assumed was Hatchet's, even though she sounded much younger, said, "Oy, Casey,"

Crippler turned to her and yelled, "You remember my name?!"

Hatchet laughed in the video, and then the video ended. "Yeah," said Hatchet as she put away the phone. "Good times."

I had realized that everyone had been laughing really hard during the video, including me. Most of us were wiping our eyes while still chuckling.

I turned to Hatchet and said, "Obviously that was before The Black Cougars."

"Yeah," said Hatchet. "Talon made the group a year after that, when we were in 8th grade."

I chuckled. "You guys seemed so innocent. You couldn't have known that you would join an outlawed group and become criminals."

"Yeah," Hatchet sighed. "Times change."

"Yup," said Blade, his mouth filled with pancake.

"Hey," I said, "do we still have some more pancakes?"

"Yup," said Hatchet. "We have three left. Do you want one?"

CHAPTER TEN

THAT DAY WAS A Saturday, so we went to the jailhouse and visited Talon for about 45 minutes. We gave him his homework to do, but we knew that we couldn't turn it in until he got back so that the teacher wouldn't be suspicious.

After that, they dropped me off at my house, but waited outside. Hatchet was driving and I walked inside and said, "Hey, mom. Can I hang out with my friends today?"

She was in the kitchen making a sandwich. She wiped off her hands on her blue apron and said, "You certainly are spending a lot of time with your new friends. I sure would like to meet them."

The blood drained from my face. "Sure," I said. "They'll, uh, be right in."

I walked outside and Hatchet said, "Well?"

I cleared my throat. "Uh, my mom wants to meet you guys."

"Okay," said Hatchet.

Just then, my mom came out of the house and started walking down the driveway until she was in front of the car.

Hatchet got out of the car and came around to the front. "Ma'am," she said and shook my mom's hand.

"Well," said my mom. "You're very polite."

"Thank you, ma'am," she said and opened up the passenger seat, which was occupied by Blade, and leaned on it with her left arm. She had taken off her puffy jacket and had put the leather jacket back on, since it had warmed up a little. She was also wearing those sunglasses that are light at the top, but then fade into dark towards the bottom. The frames were like the ones that people would sometimes wear in the '70s.

My mom said, "I like your jacket. I've always like leather." She leaned in to Hatchet and said, "Nice taste in cars, too."

"Thank you, ma'am," said Hatchet. The hood was up, but you could still tell it was a convertible.

My mom said, "Well, what's your name?"

Hatchet said, "My name is Hatchet."

My mom nodded her head and said, "That's an unusual name."

"It's a nickname, ma'am," said Hatchet.

My mom turned to me and said, "Can I meet the rest of your friends?"

Before I could answer, Hatchet said, "Certainly." She stepped aside and everybody got out of the car.

She pointed to Blade. "This is Blade."

Blade waved and said, "Hello."

Hatchet pointed to Mangle and said, "This is Mangle." She pointed to Narcissist and said, "This is Narcissist."

She went down the whole list until there was nobody left to introduce. My mom said, "Well!" She turned to me and said, "You all have such scary names." She laughed. "It doesn't matter though. You have quite the lot of friends." She turned back to them and she said, "And they all seem like lovely people."

Crippler snorted like he was going to laugh, then smiled and put his index finger under his nose. Everybody looked at him like, *Shut up.*

"What?" asked my mom, completely unaware that these were The Black Cougars.

"Nothing," said Crippler. "I just thought of something funny I saw earlier."

Blade turned to Crippler and said, "You mean that video of you spazing out earlier?"

Everybody immediately started laughing really hard. Hatchet was laughing so hard that she had to hold her stomach.

"What?" said my mom. "What's so funny?"

I turned to Hatchet like, *Can we show her?*

Hatchet nodded her head and turned around and got the

same phone from earlier out from the glove department where Blade had been sitting.

I turned to my mom, still asking, "What are you laughing about?"

I said, "This is the video that we watched earlier that everybody was laughing about."

Hatchet got it ready, then handed it to my mom and said, "Just press play." Then she got behind my mom's shoulder and everybody else crowded behind us too, wanting to see the spastic video again.

The video started and everybody started chuckling immediately. My mom was smiling, but she also looked scared. Then Crippler really started spazing out and the video had everybody rolling. The video ended and my mom gave the phone back to Hatchet, who was still chuckling and wiping her eyes again.

"Uh, here you go," said my mom as she handed back the phone. She was smiling and she was chuckling, but she also looked horrified. Then she turned to Crippler and said, "Crippler, right?"

"Yeah," said Crippler.

My mom said, "Are you okay? How can your body make spasms like that?"

Crippler just chuckled and said, "First of all, yes I am okay. Second of all, my body can do that because I have mastered the fine art of spazing out."

Everybody started laughing again, including my mom. "Okay," said my mom. "I was just making sure that you didn't sprain any body parts or anything."

"Well thank you for your consideration," said Crippler, and my mom chuckled.

My mom turned to me and said, "Now that I feel comfortable because I know who you are hanging out with, you can hang out with them."

"Thanks, mom!" I said as everyone loaded back up into the car. We pulled away and I leaned partway out the window, waved, and said, "Bye mom!"

Since there are only five seats in the car, usually we have the top down, three people have to sit on the back with their feet in the seats, and one person has to sit in the middle area between the driver and passenger seats. There are three seats in the back and two seats in the front. Because Talon wasn't there, only two people had to sit on the back. For that particular instance, Hatchet said that we had to squeeze into the back so that my mom didn't get worried. It was a little cramped, but we managed.

Now, as we pulled away, we rounded the corner so that we were out of sight and rolled down the cover. Blade squeezed out and got on top. He wiggled a little bit and said, "Much better." A few seconds later, Crippler joined him.

We started laughing and we drove away.

"Hey," said Hatchet and she turned to Blade. "Do you want to take the wheel for a while?"

"Sure," said Blade. Hatchet pulled over and switched places with Blade.

As Hatchet slipped into the passenger seat, she pulled out a book. We started driving away, and Blade looked over and asked, "What are you doing?"

Hatchet looked up, confused, and said, "Reading."

Now Blade looked confused. "What? Why?"

Hatchet, the same look on her face, said, "Because I want to."

Blade shrugged, still confused, and said, "Alright."

Hatchet looked down and continued reading.

"What are you reading?" I asked.

"*The Hidden Oracle* by Rick Riordan," Hatchet replied.

"What's it about?" asked Klepto.

"Greek and Roman mythology."

"So criminals can be geeks, too," I said, as if observing something.

I expected Hatchet to be mad at me, but she just turned around, smiling, and said, "Nice one, kid."

After about fifteen minutes, Hatchet put the book away.

"What happened?" asked Blade. "Did you get bored of it already?"

"No," said Hatchet. "I just wanted to finish the chapter I was on."

"Okay," said Blade. "Hey, do you want to switch again?"

"Why?" asked Hatchet.

"I just remembered that my driver's permit got revoked. I crashed into a fire hydrant."

Hatchet looked at him in disbelief. "Uh, yeah! Pull over right now!"

Blade pulled over and Hatchet started driving again. Blade took his place on the back and Klepto rode shotgun.

Hatchet started driving, then said, "How about we turn on some music?" She cued up Spotify on her phone and heavy metal started playing. A few minutes later, the next song started playing and Hatchet said, "Oh! This is my favorite song!" and turned it up.

"Hey," I said over the loud music. "Where are we going anyways?"

"You'll see when we get there," said Hatchet, turning down the music.

"That doesn't make me feel any better."

"It's okay," said Hatchet. "It'll be fun."

"Okay," I said. "By the way, if you can't afford very much food, then how did you get this car?"

"We stole it," said Klepto, and Hatchet punched him in the arm.

"We did not steal it. We found it in a dump. It didn't work anymore and it was dirty, but we brought it back and fixed it up."

"How?" I asked.

Klepto said, "I used to work in a machine shop fixing cars. It's actually pretty easy, once you know what to do."

"Wow," I said. "That's pretty cool."

"Yeah," said Klepto. He looked proud of himself. I know I would be if I had fixed up a broken down car, and then got to keep it.

"How did you keep the job steady?" I asked.

"I didn't," he responded. "I worked there for about six months before the owner found out I was with The Black Cougars. He fired me."

"Hey," I said to Hatchet. "How do you know which person is next in line to be leader?"

"Well," said Hatchet, "Talon was the person who made the group, so he's the first Black Cougar. Therefore, he's the leader. If something were to happen to him that forced him to leave the group or something, then I would be the leader because I've been around the longest. Now, if something were to happen to me, then Blade would become the leader. After Blade is kind of tricky, though. Since Mangle and Klepto were brought to the group at the same time, then Mangle would become the leader because he's older."

"Not mentally," said Klepto in a whiny voice. Mangle punched him in the arm, and Klepto smiled.

"Anyways," said Hatchet, "Mangle would be leader, then

Klepto, then Narcissist, then E.L., then Crippler, then finally you, Lore."

I'm not exactly sure why, but this came as a surprise to me. "Wait, so you mean I'll be leader one day?"

"Maybe," said Hatchet, "I mean, no offense, but hopefully not, because that means that something would happen to the person before you, and we don't want that to happen. But otherwise, yeah maybe."

"Cool," I said.

The conversation was over, so Hatchet pumped up the music again and we drove in silence, listening to heavy metal.

CHAPTER ELEVEN

WE DROVE FOR A while and went through a lot of songs. Four different hard rock songs played and the fourth one was my favorite. We pulled up at an amusement park just as another hard rock song started playing.

"What are we doing here?" I asked.

Hatchet turned to me with a grin on her face and said, "Here we are."

Everybody cheered and got out of the car excitedly. E.L., Blade, and Klepto all raced to the front gates. E.L. won and Blade and Klepto started arguing that it wasn't fair and that she got a head start.

E.L. turned to Hatchet and said, "Come on! Hurry up!"

"Be patient!" Hatchet yelled back. E.L. groaned.

"What is this place?" I asked.

"It's an old abandoned amusement park," said Narcissist.

"Yeah, I got that part," I said.

Narcissist said, "It may be old and abandoned, but last year we found it and we fixed everything up. The rides are all fully functional now, and there's no wait."

"Really?" I said. Now I was getting excited, too. "Who fixed it up?"

"The same person who fixed up the car." Narcissist pointed to Klepto, who was busy tugging on the gates, still waiting for Hatchet to come over.

"Wow," I said. "He learned a lot from working in that machine shop."

"Yeah, no kidding," said Narcissist.

"How long did it take him to fix up everything?" I asked.

"About a week."

"How many rides are there?"

"I have no idea." Narcissist chuckled as she ran over to the gates with everyone else.

I also ran over to the gates and joined everyone else. Hatchet finally came over to the gates and said, "Why are you guys waiting? You know I don't have a key. Just jump over like always."

"Oh yeah!" said Klepto as if he had just remembered this. Everyone pulled out a pair of black leather gloves and put them on. Klepto was the first over. He put on his gloves, gripped the bars, and pulled himself up without using his legs at all. He made it to the top, which was about seven feet off the ground, then pulled his legs up so that he was sitting on top of the gates and turned to the other side and jumped down. Everyone else did the same.

After everyone was over, it was only Hatchet and I that were left on the other side. Hatchet pulled out her gloves and started putting them on. She turned to me and said, "Oh! You need gloves, don't you?" She reached into her jacket and pulled out a pair of gloves for me.

I grabbed the gloves and said, "Why do we have to wear gloves?"

Hatchet pulled her glove on like they do in movies where they put their hand straight up and pull down on the glove and wiggle their fingers. Then she pointed to the gate and said, "See the rust?"

I looked at the gate. It was really rusty. The parts that weren't covered with rust were green. "Yeah?" I said.

Hatchet put down her hand and said, "If you cut your hand on that, you'll get tetanus. And you don't want tetanus. Blade got it last year, and he had lockjaw for a week until we got enough money to take him to the doctor to give him shots."

"Ouch," I said. "That sounds painful."

"It was painful to look at." Hatchet gripped the gates. "Come on."

After Hatchet had made it over, I put on my gloves and started hoisting myself up the gate. Klepto made it look so easy. It was actually really hard to pull myself up with just my arms. I lifted my leg up to try and climb up by pushing the bars, but my foot slipped and I almost fell.

Now I know why they use only their arms. I thought.

I made it all the way to the top, and then jumped down and everybody started cheering for me.

"Her first break-in," said Klepto, pretending to wipe a tear from his eye. "I'm so proud."

Hatchet punched him in the arm, laughing, and then turned around and said, "Let's go."

We walked up to the first ride called, "TNT" (short for Twists N' Turns), which looked dangerous, but Klepto assured me it was fully operational.

E.L., Hatchet, Mangle, and I got on. Electrical Line sat next to me in the very front car and Hatchet and Mangle sat together in the seat behind us. Klepto pulled the lever to start the ride.

The ride took off very fast and went through lots of twists and turns. We went through a tunnel at one point, and we went over the whole park. When the starting point was in view again, Klepto started pulling back on the lever, slowing us down until we came to a stop exactly where we were when we got on.

I got off and almost fell over. "That was awesome!" I said.

Blade and Klepto got in the first row and Narcissist and Crippler sat in the car behind them. Hatchet pulled the lever to start the ride.

I counted in my head. *One, two, three . . .* I got to around thirty when they got back.

They were all smiling and laughing. "Can we go again?" I asked.

"Maybe at the end," said Narcissist. "First, we have to go on the other rides."

The next ride was called Loop Around and it had five different loops. I asked not to go on that one.

"Why?" asked E.L.

"I don't like loops," I said. "They're scary for me."

"That's okay," said E.L. "You don't have to go on this one."

The ride after that that we went on was called, "Two-Faced". There were two tracks that wound around each other. This one everyone went on, half on one side and half on the other. I was in the very front seat again on the left track with Narcissist next to me on my right. E.L. and Crippler were in the row behind us, Crippler on the left and E.L. on the right. Hatchet was next to Klepto in the front row on the right track. Klepto said that he had to be on the right side of the row to reach the controls. Blade and Mangle were in the row behind them, Blade on the left and Mangle on the right.

Klepto leaned over to a big box and pressed a button. All the lap bars came down and a voice came over the loudspeaker: "Five, four, three, two, one." On "one," the ride took off.

It was slightly slower than the very first one we went on, but it was still pretty fast. The tracks wound around each other, except for when we went through a tunnel. In the tunnel, there was a mirror on either side. When we came out, Blade's eyes were wide and he wasn't smiling anymore. He was covering his forehead. Then I realized his bandana was gone.

The rest of the ride continued with lots of turns and winding around tracks. The whole time, Blade never uncovered his forehead. When we got off, Blade went up to Klepto and said, "Is there any way to access the tracks?"

"What do you mean?" asked Klepto with a confused look on his face.

"I mean can you walk on it?" asked Blade, still covering his forehead.

"Yeah, I guess," replied Klepto. "Why?"

"I lost my bandana."

"Okay," said Klepto. He turned around to everyone and said, "Hey, guys! We have to go on the track. Look for Blade's bandana!"

Everybody squeezed past the roller coaster car and started walking on the tracks.

"Where did you lose it?" asked Klepto.

"In the tunnel," said Blade, desperately looking for his bandana.

What is with him and that bandana? I wondered.

We kept walking all the way up to the tunnel. We were searching there, when Blade said, "I found it!" He held it up, then turned around and put it back on, making sure to tie it tightly. He turned back around, and he had a relieved look on his face.

"All right!" said Klepto, his voice echoing in the tunnel. "Everybody back to the beginning of the ride!"

We made it back to the beginning of the ride safely. Everybody stepped off, then headed off to the next ride.

"Hey, Blade," I said because Blade was towards the back of the group.

"Yeah?" he responded.

"Why were you so worried about finding your bandana?" I asked.

Blade's face turned pale. "I just really like it, okay?"

"That's what you said last time. Tell me the truth."

"Look, I don't want to talk about it, alright?" Blade said with frustration in his voice.

"But -"

"I said I don't want to talk about it, okay?" Blade jogged up to the rest of the group and put his arms around Klepto and Mangle. They started joking around and laughing. Blade looked back at me once, like he was worried that I might yell out, "Hey guys, Blade's insecure about taking his bandana off and he won't tell me why!"

Anyways, we arrived at the next ride. It was called, "Bonkers". So far, all of the names had coordinated with the way the rides were, so I was a little scared to try this one out.

We got up to the roller coaster and Klepto said, "Everyone can go on this one."

Everybody cheered and filed into the rows. I, again, was in the first row (I think it was because it was my first time here, so they let me be in the front), with Mangle sitting to my left. Behind me was Klepto, with Narcissist to his left. Then there was Blade on the right and Hatchet on the left, and finally, E.L. on the right and Crippler on the left.

Klepto leaned over and flipped a switch on the control panel. While we were waiting for the ride to start, Klepto leaned over to Mangle and said, "Hey, Mangle. Wouldn't it suck if the brakes stopped working so we just came crashing through the end?" Klepto had started laughing halfway through the sentence, and he also had started demonstrating with his hand.

I got worried. "Has that happened before?" I asked.

Klepto grinned and said, "Not yet."

I turned around and the ride started up. Everyone immediately put their hands up and started cheering. I soon found out why it was called Bonkers. The ride jerked this way and that, twisting and turning, lurching side to side. It was fun, though.

After we got off, I was a little dizzy. I stumbled around and fell into Mangle.

"Hey," he said, "Are you okay?"

"Yeah," I said, the world spinning before my eyes. "I'm just dizzy."

"Yeah," said Hatchet. "Everybody's like that their first time on this ride. Sometimes even the fourth or fifth time after that!"

Everybody looked at Crippler.

Crippler whined, "Ah, come on, guys!"

Blade just looked at him and said, "Dude, you threw up."

"Come on, man!" Crippler said. "That was one time!"

Narcissist came over to me and said, "Here, I'll help you to the next ride."

Narcissist put her arm around me and supported me a little bit. I put my arm around her so I wouldn't fall down. She helped me to the next ride, and by then I wasn't dizzy anymore, so I got on the ride by myself.

This one was called, "Claim Jumper", so I didn't really know what to expect. Only half of us could get on, because it was another one of the lever operated ones, and they decided that it would be mean to make Klepto ride all alone.

Half of us got on, and Klepto pulled back the lever. The ride didn't start off that fast, but it did start going up a hill. It took about five to seven seconds to get to the top, and the hill was pretty steep. We got to the top and I looked down. I could feel my face turn into an expression of terror. The hill was very steep, and it was probably the biggest hill I had ever been on. We started going down, and everybody screamed, though I saw the hands go up in the back, and I suspected that the screams I was hearing were happy screams.

The whole ride was just big bumps. None of them were as big as the one at the beginning, but they were still a pretty good size. At the end, I had tears in my eyes from how much wind had gone in my face.

I got off the ride and Klepto was smiling. When he saw my tears, he said, "Are you okay? What's wrong?"

"Nothing," I said, wiping my eyes. "It's just from the wind."

Klepto sighed. "Okay. Just checking."

The other half of The Black Cougars got on, and Hatchet pulled back the lever.

They actually started off faster than it felt, and they started climbing the mountain. When they got to the top, they stopped for about two seconds, then the ride continued. I could hear their faint screams.

About forty-five seconds later, the ride ended and they got off the ride, laughing. I surveyed everyone and realized that I was the only one so far who had started tearing up because of the wind. It made me feel kind of weird.

"Hey," I said to Klepto. "Why was I the only one who started tearing up because of the wind?"

Klepto grabbed his chin and put his elbow in his hand. He furrowed his eyebrows. "I'm not sure. Maybe you have sensitive eyes."

"Yeah, that sounds like me," I said, nodding my head. We both started laughing.

Klepto turned around to everyone and spread his arms. "Okay, off to the next ride!" he announced.

We stayed there the whole day, and all the rides were so fun! At the end, when we were walking to the gates to go home I asked, "Hey, what is this place called?"

Hatchet furrowed her eyebrows. "You know, I don't think this place has a name. We've always referred to it as, 'The Amusement Park'."

I thought for a little bit. "Ooh! Maybe we could call it 'Black Cougar Land'."

Hatchet thought about it. She shrugged her shoulders. "I don't have a better idea." She turned to the rest of The Black Cougars and said, "Black Cougars! I have an announcement! I hereby dub this abandoned amusement park . . .Black Cougar Land!"

Everybody cheered.

Hatchet said, "By the way, Lore came up with the idea." She gestured at me with her thumb.

Everybody cheered again and high-fived me. "Great job, Lore!" they said.

"Thanks," I said. I was kind of proud of myself.

We kept walking towards the gates, and everyone put on their gloves again. I realized that Hatchet had never taken my gloves back, so I patted down my jacket for them. I found them in my left pocket and pulled them out. I put them on, and one by one we went back over the gate.

When we got into the car, the first thing Hatchet did was turn on the radio and immediately turned down the music. The song turned on about five seconds after the car started up, so Hatchet was right to turn it down immediately. It was still playing the same hard rock song as when we had gotten out of the car. We started driving and I asked, "Where are we going?"

Hatchet turned around, which did not reassure my safety, and she said, "We're going to the clearing. We're going to sit around the fire and tell stories."

"Cool!" I said.

"Oh yeah," said Narcissist. "You've never been to a BCC have you?"

"What's a BCC?" I asked.

"It stands for Black Cougar Campfire," explained Narcissist. "We call it a campfire because, usually, people only tell ghost stories and stuff by a campfire."

"Yeah," said E.L. "It's SO much fun. You have to come!"

"I'll text my mom right now," I said. I got out my phone and opened up my text messaging app. *Can I stay with my friends a little late again tonight?* My mom texted back, *As long as you come back by dinnertime. Love you.* Then she sent a kissy face emoji.

I turned off my phone and put it back in my jacket.

"What did she say?" asked E.L.

"She said yeah," I said and everyone cheered.

"Yeah!" said Hatchet and she turned up the music, which had turned to another heavy metal song.

CHAPTER TWELVE

WE DROVE THE REST of the way smiling and listening to music. The songs showed some variety of bands. After the heavy metal song, there was an alternative rock song, then another hard rock song, then a classic rock song, and just as we pulled up to the clearing, another alternative rock song started playing. When the classic rock song started playing, I turned to Hatchet and said, "I thought you said we had to listen to heavy metal bands."

"Yeah, Talon likes to tell them that, but you don't have to," said Hatchet. "You just can't listen to girly pop music."

"Oh," I said. "Okay."

The song was actually pretty good. Anyways, we got out of the car and Hatchet pulled the matches out from her pocket. She scraped the match against the packet, but it didn't catch. She tried a few more times, then just gave up and pulled a new one out. She lit it and threw it into the trashcan, which immediately caught on fire (the inside, I mean).

"How do you do that?" I asked.

"What do you mean?" asked Hatchet.

"I mean, how do you catch the trashcan on fire so easily? Is it drenched in gasoline or something?"

"Actually, yes," said Hatchet.

"Oh," I said. "Okay. That makes sense now."

We swapped stories around the fire and were laughing the whole time. Afterwards, they drove me home for the night.

The next few days while Talon was in jail were fairly uneventful. We started hanging out with the other Black Cougars more – Cramer, Thompson, and Taylor – because I pointed out to the rest of the group that they might feel left out. I pointed out that they were part of the group too, so we should acknowledge that. They also gave the moles names, too, so Cramer became Canon, Thompson became Terrible, and Taylor became Neglect.

After the few days were over *all* of The Black Cougars – including the three information moles – went to the jailhouse to see Talon get out of jail. Everyone was so excited to finally see him out and healthy.

He came out dressed exactly the same as when he had gone in. He came out and everybody cheered. We ran up and hugged him. He hugged back.

He looked at us and said, "It's good to see you guys."

He noticed that the moles were there and he said, "Hey! Cramer, Thompson, Taylor! What are you guys doing here?" He sounded pleasantly surprised.

I explained to him what I had told the rest of the group about the moles. After I was done Talon's eyes went big. He turned to the moles and said, "Guys, I didn't even realize that you might have felt that way. I'm sorry."

Thompson, now known as Terrible, blew her lips and waved away the comment. "It's no big deal. It does feel good to be a part of the actual group, though."

Cramer, now Canon, and Taylor, now Neglect, agreed.

"Hey!" said Hatchet, "Your leg healed up! Looks like those two weeks in jail did you some good, eh?" she said, gently punching him in the shoulder.

Talon laughed. "Yeah. Hey, guys, how was having Hatchet as the leader?"

Mangle said, "HORRIBLE."

Hatchet punched him in the arm.

Mangle laughed and said, "Nah, it wasn't that bad. We do prefer you, though."

Everybody agreed.

Talon smiled and said, "Where are the keys?"

Hatchet pulled them out of her right pocket. She tossed them to Talon and said, "Here. Why?"

Talon held up the keys and said, "Because I haven't driven

you guys anywhere in two weeks. My leg works again, so I'm driving."

Everybody laughed and got into the car, Talon in the driver's seat and Hatchet in the passenger seat. Terrible had to sit in the middle up front, and a few people had to sit on the floor in the back, since Talon said the most people on the back of the car could be three, not six. Talon rubbed his hands on the steering wheel. "This feels good," he said. With a smile, he started up the ignition.

We drove to the clearing. Everybody got out of the car and Talon started up a fire in the trashcan. He sighed. "I missed doing that."

"We all did," said Mangle.

We sat around the fire and talked for a little while, and Talon got mad when he found out that he had missed my first trip to Black Cougar Land and my first BCC.

Hatchet laughed and said, "By the way, Talon, we saved up our money again and bought a few more sleeping bags. You know what that means."

Talon grinned. "Campout."

Everyone cheered. We got the sleeping bags out of the truck. Everyone got situated with their sleeping partner. Mine was Mangle. Everybody kept their jackets on since it was a little crisp that night.

We all settled down into our sleeping bags, and everyone

said goodnight to each other. We all went to sleep, happy that Talon was back.

I woke up to find Blade trying to wake up Talon, but Talon was a deep sleeper. Everybody else woke up, too. They started mumbling and asking each other questions.

Talon finally woke up. He rubbed his eyes and yawned. "What's wrong?" he asked.

Blade looked worried. His face was pale.

Talon started getting worried, too. "Blade, what's wrong?" he said in a calm, but stern voice.

Blade took a deep breath and readied himself, then finally spoke. "Hatchet's gone."

Printed in the United States
By Bookmasters